What do the fairies do with all those teeth?

To Joachim and Nicholas

A FIREFLY BOOK

Published in the U.S. in 1996 by:
Firefly Books (U.S.) Inc.
P.O. Box 1338
Ellicott Station
Buffalo, New York 14207

6 5 4 3 2 1   Printed in Canada   6 7 8 9/9

Cataloguing in Publication Data

Luppens, Michel, 1950-
  [Mais que font les fées avec toutes ces dents?
English]
  What do the fairies do with all those teeth?

Translation of: Mais que font les fées avec toutes
ces dents?
ISBN 1-55209-001-9 (bound). — ISBN 1-55209-002-7 (pbk.)

1. Picture books for children. I. Béha, Philippe.
II. Title. III. Title: Mais que font les fées avec toutes
ces dents? English.

PS8573.U66M3313 1996   jC843'.54   C95-932463-1
PZ7.L8Wh 1996

What do the fairies do with all those teeth?

MICHEL LUPPENS

English text by
JANE BRIERLEY

PHILIPPE BÉHA

FIREFLY BOOKS

Losing your first tooth is an important event.

They say if you hide it under your pillow, a tooth fairy comes in the night and takes it, leaving behind a few coins or a little gift.

But have you ever wondered what the fairies *do* with all those teeth?

YES! WHAT DO THEY DO?

Do they collect them just for the fun of it?

Do they string them into necklaces?

Do they choose the sharpest teeth to make their saws?

Or the roundest ones to make maraca sounds?

Perhaps they just make sets of false teeth?

Unless they choose the longest ones
to make their Halloween disguises?

Or the brightest to grind up into stardust . . .

Who knows? Maybe they take the most decayed, and get some witch to make a magic potion...

And by the way, do the fairies
just collect *children's* teeth?

WHAT IF THEY VISIT
THE ANIMALS, TOO...?

LUP   Luppens, Michel

**What do the fair-
ies do with all
those teeth?**

DUE DATE